Peryton Panic

Peryton Panic

by Penumbra Quill

Little, Brown and Company
New York Boston

Little, Brown and Company
Hachette Book Group
1290 Avenue of the Americas, New York, NY 10104
Visit us at LBYR.com
mylittlepony.com

First Edition: January 2018

Little, Brown and Company is a division of Hachette Book Group, Inc. The Little, Brown name and logo are trademarks of Hachette Book Group, Inc.

The publisher is not responsible for websites (or their content) that are not owned by the publisher.

Library of Congress Control Number 2017954680

ISBNs: 978-0-316-55743-6 (pbk.), 978-0-316-55741-2 (ebook)

Printed in the United States of America

LSC-C

10 9 8 7 6 5 4 3 2 1

The Pony was *not* pleased. That meddling Princess Twilight always poked her muzzle where it didn't belong. And where the annoying Alicorn went, her equally frustrating friends followed. If The Pony didn't act soon, moons of careful planning would be lost, and the Livewood would remain closed forever. The time for caution had passed. Now, it was time to set magic into motion.

The Pony poured a glowing elixir into the dirt at the barrier of the Livewood. As the drops of liquid hit the soil of the Everfree Forest, the ground churned. Now it would be ready to accept the seeds The Pony had cultivated for just this purpose. Thank the Pony of Shadows that those bumbling Cutie

Mark Crusaders had knocked over the fear fern in the greenhouse instead of *this* plant. The trembling forest floor grew still once again, with only a slight golden shine to show where the potion had fallen.

Blue Moon used his magic to place each starburst-shaped seed into the gleaming dirt. With a nudge of his power, the seeds burrowed deep into the earth. The moment of destiny had come. From this point on, there would be no turning back.

CHAPTER ONE

Sweetie Belle had never played tag with a Phoenix before. She giggled as the flame-colored bird squawked a *"you can't catch me!"* before flapping deeper into the Everfree Forest. She chased after him through the huge trees, ducking under their outstretched branches. But as Sweetie Belle reached a clearing, the Phoenix was nowhere to be seen.

"Guess I lost *that* game." She shrugged.

"Eeeyup," came a familiar voice behind her. Sweetie Belle turned, surprised to see Big Mac nearby. She had thought she was the only pony in the Forest today. Apple Bloom and Scootaloo had been too busy wallpapering Cranky Doodle's new tree house, so they'd decided not to come along on her adventure.

Big Mac kicked a tree, and zap apples floated down from it, landing in a perfect stack in his basket.

"Do you need some help?" Sweetie Belle asked.

"That's ever so kind of you to offer, Sweetie Belle," Big Mac said, speaking in a cultured accent—a lot like Rarity's, Sweetie Belle realized. "But I am not the creature who is seeking your assistance. There are times when one must look beyond what one sees, you know. Some things are clearer in darkness. Fireflies, for example."

As though the word had summoned them, fireflies flitted down from the trees and swirled around Sweetie Belle in a flickering dance.

"I'm not sure I understand," she told Big Mac. Or at least, it *had* been Big Mac. Now he had horns sprouting from his head and a long beard.

"Look to the leaves." Big Mac/Not Big Mac winked, gesturing with a now paw-shaped front foot.

Sweetie Belle watched as the Forest's carpet of fallen foliage began to shift, as though under the weight of an invisible four-footed creature. A path of odd hoofprints appeared ahead of her. Well, some of them were hoofprints. The others looked as if they had been made by...talons?

"Don't forget your turnip-and-spaghetti raincoat," Big Mac called after her before stretching his wings and flying off.

Now, that was weird. Wasn't it? Sweetie Belle thought as she got on a pink-striped pogo stick and bounced down the footprint trail. It took a few more hops across a field of singing sunflowers before she realized that this had to be a dream.

And if she *knew* it was a dream...that

must mean Princess Luna was nearby. At least, Sweetie Belle thought, that's what had happened every *other* time she'd realized she was dreaming. Maybe Luna wanted to talk to her. It must be lonely being the Princess of Night, Sweetie Belle thought, staying awake when everypony was asleep.

"Princess Luna? Hello? Are you here?" Sweetie Belle called, looking around.

But there was no answer. And suddenly, everything shifted. The sunshine and warmth of the Forest was gone. In the sky, the sun had dwindled to a tiny, glowing ring of light covered almost entirely by shadow. It was an eclipse, Sweetie Belle realized. An icy wind whipped past her flank, and she shivered.

At the sound of crunching leaves behind her, Sweetie Belle turned.

"Luna?" she whispered.

It wasn't Luna.

Sweetie Belle watched in terror as a fearsome creature stepped toward her. It tossed its huge head, and sharp, enormous antlers gleamed like silver in the faint light. Flaming white eyes burned in its shadowy face, and wings made of smoke unfurled from its back. Then, with a rush faster than she could blink, the beast leaped at her!

WHAM! Sweetie Belle hit the floor, screaming. She pounded her hooves against the creature's silk hide. Wait. Silk?

Sweetie Belle opened her eyes to find she was on the floor of her room, battling her own bedsheets. Embarrassed, she realized she must have fallen out of bed when she woke up from her dream-turned-nightmare.

And suddenly, her bedroom door flew open. Rarity rushed in, her sleeping mask pushed up over her horn and her mane in curlers.

"Sweetie Belle, darling! I heard you screaming! Is everything all right?" Rarity asked, shining a globe of magical light around the room.

"I...had a nightmare," Sweetie Belle admitted.

Rarity smoothed Sweetie's mane with a gentle big-sister smile.

"Well, fortunately, I know just the thing for those!" Rarity soothed, returning in a moment with two steaming cups of chamomile tea. "Now, I know it's been *ages* and you're much too grown up for it. But perhaps, just for tonight, I might sing the rose song?"

Sweetie Belle nodded and sipped her tea. That lullaby always made her feel safe.

The two sisters snuggled up together, and Rarity began to sing. *"A rose has thorns to keep it safe, but ponies have not one. A wild rose blooms where it is placed, but ponies seek the sun. A rose is sweet and beautiful . . ."* Rarity trailed off.

"Its scent is lush and rare . . ." Sweetie Belle prompted. But she quickly realized that Rarity hadn't forgotten the words. . . . She'd just fallen asleep. Sweetie Belle pulled up the covers and tried to drift off, too. But every time she closed her eyes, she saw the creature in her mind. And it felt as if it were watching her.

CHAPTER TWO

Sweetie Belle yawned widely.

"Crooked cattails, Sweetie Belle, stop yawnin'!" Apple Bloom complained, her own jaws gaping in response. "Those things are downright contagious!" Scootaloo nodded as she yawned, too.

"Sorry," Sweetie Belle said. After her nightmare last night, she'd been too afraid to get much sleep. But she couldn't tell her friends that. Ever since she had faced down the werepony-Timberwolf version of Twist, all Ponyville thought she was brave. She didn't want to change their minds. She *liked* not being called a scaredy-pony.

"You really think this'll work?" Scootaloo asked as the Cutie Mark Crusaders made their way to Fluttershy's animal sanctuary.

"Of course it will!" Apple Bloom enthused. "Fluttershy's gonna love Lilymoon and Ambermoon once she gets ta know 'em like we do!"

Sweetie Belle wasn't so sure. Twilight Sparkle had made it pretty clear that the Moon family was mixed up in some dangerous magic. Ever since they'd moved into the spooky house atop Horseshoe Hill, strange things had been happening around Ponyville. First the bogle attacked the Schoolhouse, then Twist turned into a Timberwolf, next the Olden Pony terrorized the town...and every single one of those events was somehow related to Lilymoon and Ambermoon. But the Cutie Mark Crusaders had decided that their new friends deserved a chance to prove their innocence to Twilight. Which was where Apple Bloom's plan came in...

"Fluttershy is the nicest pony we know.

When she sees how helpful Lilymoon and Ambermoon are at her animal sanctuary, she'll tell Twilight. Then, they can help Applejack with the harvest and Pinkie Pie with bakin', and soon everypony will see how great they are!" Apple Bloom enthused.

Sweetie Belle knew it was no use—once Apple Bloom came up with an idea, she never seemed to think of all the things that could go wrong. Fortunately, Scootaloo did.

"But *we're* not even sure we can trust Lilymoon and Ambermoon," Scootaloo said. "I mean, they're our friends and all, but they still haven't told us the whole story about their family."

"Well, this is a nice surprise," came a soft voice. The Cutie Mark Crusaders jumped, startled to see Fluttershy smiling at them. They had all been so deep in conversation, Sweetie Belle hadn't realized they'd reached the Sweet Feather Sanctuary. "I'd love to invite you in for tea, but today's bath day," Fluttershy explained gently. "I have a lot of animals to wash, and I don't want any of them to get cold waiting around." Angel Bunny nodded impatiently, a shower cap on his ears and a towel around his waist.

"That's why we're here," Apple Bloom said cheerfully. "We thought you might need a few extra hooves to pitch in!"

"Oh, how thoughtful." Fluttershy beamed. "That would be wonderful!" But when Ambermoon and Lilymoon arrived a few moments later, Sweetie Belle saw Fluttershy's smile shrink. "Are . . . you here to help, too?" Fluttershy asked nervously.

"*Mm-hm!* They *love* animals! In fact, Lilymoon got her cutie mark 'cause she's so good with creatures!" Apple Bloom said. Sweetie Belle and Scootaloo nodded enthusiastically.

"I didn't know that," Fluttershy said kindly. "Well, it *would* be nice to have some help today. Baths always take longer than you expect. Especially when the otters insist on playing in the mud as soon as you get them clean."

"My cutie mark is for *supernatural* creatures," Lilymoon whispered to the CMCs as they followed Fluttershy into the animal sanctuary.

Apple Bloom shrugged. "I didn't think we needed to mention that part just yet."

Bathtubs of all shapes and sizes were set up on the sanctuary lawn. Ducks floated happily in buckets. A line of gerbils waited their turn at a tiny diving board into a small basin. Harry the bear growled with contentment as he snuggled deeper into his bubble bath, foam up to his nose. Piles of fluffy towels and sweet-smelling soaps were arrayed nearby.

Sweetie Belle was surprised to see every kind of bathing tool imaginable—from extra-long-handled scrub brushes for giraffe necks to soft moss washcloths for lizard scales.

Fluttershy assigned each pony an animal to bathe, and soon the CMCs were scrubbing fur alongside Lilymoon and Ambermoon. Sweetie Belle lovingly poured lavender shampoo on Lola the sloth's fur. Apple Bloom was having a little more trouble wrangling Winnie the hedgehog, who apparently didn't like bath day.

"Sorry we were late," Lilymoon said when Fluttershy was out of earshot. "It took us longer to get out of the house than we expected."

"She *means* Mother doesn't want us to see you anymore," Ambermoon said flatly.

CHAPTER THREE

"What?" Sweetie Belle squeaked. The Cutie Mark Crusaders gaped. The duck in Scootaloo's tub quacked indignantly.

"Why?" Apple Bloom asked.

"Princess Twilight Sparkle dragged our whole family in for a lecture about unsafe magic." Lilymoon rolled her eyes. "She practically blamed our parents for everything bad that's ever happened in Ponyville. You can see why they aren't too thrilled with us being your friends."

"But that's not our fault!" Scootaloo pointed out.

Before Lilymoon could reply, a loud roar split the air. The ponies turned to see Harry the bear, standing in his tub, teeth bared. He was obviously upset about something, thought

Sweetie Belle, but she couldn't tell what. Maybe the water had gotten cold?

"What's up with him?" Scootaloo frowned.

Sweetie Belle peered closer at Harry. His eyes were tracking...something. Sweetie Belle thought it might be a moving shadow, but then she blinked, and there was nothing there. Harry the bear swiped his paws at empty air. Sweetie Belle thought for a moment that she heard bells chiming...but that was silly. Why would there be bells out among the bathtubs?

Now the other animals in the sanctuary were growing agitated, chirping, snarling, braying, and howling.

"Something's scaring the animals," Lilymoon said. Scootaloo's duck quacked in panic and flapped its wings violently as it flew out of its bath, splashing the ponies with sudsy water.

"Ya think?" Ambermoon said, shaking her wet mane.

Like a furry tide, the creatures poured out of their tubs. Goats bounded away in a sloshing stampede. The gerbils abandoned their diving board, scampering to hide in the nearby bushes. Apple Bloom was nearly knocked over as a wave of fleeing mice mobbed her in their rush to escape. Sweetie Belle looked down to see that even Lola the sloth was trying to get away, although very slowly.

"Oh no! What's wrong?!" Fluttershy cried as she flew over, her hooves full of fresh towels. "Stop! Wait!" she called to the fleeing animals. "You'll get yourselves dirty again!"

But it was too late. The once-peaceful sanctuary was a shambles of upturned tubs and muddy grass. Fluttershy turned to the younger ponies, and Sweetie Belle could tell she was deeply upset.

"I think maybe you two should go home," Fluttershy said softly to Lilymoon and Ambermoon. The sisters looked at her in hurt surprise.

"But...they didn't do anything wrong!" Sweetie Belle protested.

"It's okay, Sweetie Belle," Lilymoon said, flipping her blue-and-white mane to hide her eyes.

"Yes. We know when we're not wanted," Ambermoon added acidly. "Come along, Lilymoon." Together, the sisters turned their backs on Fluttershy and walked off.

"I'm sorry," Fluttershy told the Cutie Mark Crusaders. "It's just that the animals have never been scared like this before. And the only new thing in my sanctuary was...them."

CHAPTER FOUR

Sweetie Belle didn't suspect anything when
Rarity invited the Cutie Mark Crusaders to
Twilight's castle for dinner that night. But as
soon as she walked in and saw that Starlight
Glimmer, Spike, Rainbow Dash, Applejack,
Rarity, Pinkie Pie, *and* Fluttershy were there,
Sweetie Belle knew what was really going on.
It was a sisterly advice ambush.

Sweetie Belle glanced at Apple Bloom and
Scootaloo. From the sour looks on their faces,
it seemed as if they had come to the same
conclusion.

"Rarity…" Sweetie Belle hissed. "I
thought you said this was just a fun dinner…."

"And it is, darling," Rarity said, batting
her eyelashes innocently. "It's simply that…
Well, we've been worried about you three.

You haven't been keeping the—how shall I say this?—safest company."

Sweetie Belle stomped her front hoof and opened her mouth to remind Rarity that *honesty* was one of the elements of friendship, but Twilight smoothly cut in.

"I'm glad you're all here. After speaking to Blue Moon, Lumi Nation, and Auntie Eclipse, I'm a little concerned that they're involved in some dangerous magic. They might not even realize it! But until I get some answers, I think it's best for everypony if we all give the Moon family some space."

"Whaddya mean?" Apple Bloom asked.

"She *means* we don't want you fillies hangin' around with Ambermoon and Lilymoon anymore. Sorry, sugarcube," Applejack told her little sister.

"What about loyalty?" Sweetie Belle burst out. "And kindness?" The older ponies looked at her in surprise. She glared at them. "It's not very *generous* to turn our backs on our new friends!"

"*Ooh, ooh*, do my element!" Pinkie Pie said, bouncing in place.

"Um . . . it's really hard to share laughter when you're not allowed to talk to somepony?" Sweetie Belle shrugged.

"I understand, and you make a good point," Twilight told Sweetie Belle sincerely. "But the element I'm worried about is *magic*. And the way things have been going, I'm afraid being friends with Lilymoon and Ambermoon puts you at a greater risk."

"But that's not fair!" Scootaloo protested.

"We're *trying* to protect you!" Rainbow Dash asserted. "Weird things keep happening! And we don't want them happening to you! Who knows what'll be next?"

"I think we're about to find out," Spike

said drily as a frantic Granny Smith raced into the dining room.

"It was horrible!" Granny panted. "The worst thing I ever saw since the frost beetles ate three quarters of the orchard!"

"Slow down, Granny. Take a deep breath. Now. What was horrible?" Applejack said, putting a hoof on Granny's shoulder.

"Quit jabberin' and listen!" Granny scowled, knocking Applejack's hoof away. "I ain't a frail flower to be coddled and swaddled. I had just tucked down fer my nap. It was nice 'n' dark, and I had my fav'rite pillow, the one cousin Tart Pippin gave me for Hearth's Warming." Granny closed her eyes, miming snuggling into a pillow.

After a few moments, Sweetie Belle wondered if Granny had really fallen asleep. She jumped when Granny's eyes flew open!

"That's when I saw it! A *huuuuuge* beast,

movin' in the shadows! And it kept makin' this horrible ringin' noise I could feel all the way down to my teeth!" Granny took out her dentures and shook them to illustrate.

"Ew," whispered Scootaloo.

"Uh, Granny? Ya don't suppose that was just yer alarm clock?" Applejack said with a patience that made Sweetie Belle think they'd had this conversation before.

"Of course it was my alarm clock!" Granny retorted. "Alarmin' me to get outta there before that beastie took a bite of Apple!"

"We'll look into it, Granny," Twilight reassured her. "Applejack, why don't you take her home and make sure everything's safe on the farm?" Applejack nodded and hustled Granny to the door.

"*Hmph.* I know a shadow creature when I see one!" Granny huffed as Applejack escorted her out. "You can tell 'cause-a their eyes. Like white fires a-*burrrrrnin'* in their sockets!"

Sweetie Belle frowned. That sounded familiar. Like something she'd once seen in a dream...

"Plus they smell like corn custard!" Granny's voice went on as she left.

"We were makin' corn custard yesterday," Apple Bloom whispered to her friends. "The whole farmhouse smells like it now. I think Granny just had a nightmare."

The older ponies turned back to the CMCs. Sweetie Belle could tell that more lectures were on the menu before dinner.

"Look, you know Twilight believes in giving ponies second chances," Starlight Glimmer said with a half smile that made Sweetie Belle realize the Unicorn was talking about herself. "Just take a little break from

Lilymoon and Ambermoon until we can figure out what's going on."

"Uh, Twilight?" Applejack walked back in with Granny. Sweetie Belle thought both ponies had a strange look on their faces. "You probably should see this."

Twilight curiously trotted over to a window, the others following her.

Sweetie Belle peered over Rarity's shoulder to see. Outside the castle, a small group of ponies had formed, and they were yelling and hammering on the front door.

"A huge creature attacked me!"

"Something's terrorizing Ponyville!"

"We're *doooooomed!*"

CHAPTER FIVE

They were never going to get dinner, Sweetie Belle realized. Twilight and her friends had been interviewing the distraught ponies to try to figure out what was going on in Ponyville. And it seemed as if each of them had a different story. Octavia Melody had complained that some creature had ruined her cello practice by insisting on playing handbells right outside her window. Bulk Biceps said a huge creature made of boxes tried to attack him. And Lotus Blossom reported that a shadow had chased her all the way across Ponyville. Sweetie Belle sighed. At least nopony could hear her stomach growling over Lyra and Bon Bon's argument.

"I'm telling you, it was a chimera!" Lyra said. "I saw goat hoofprints in the garden!"

Bon Bon rolled her eyes. "Chimeras *also* have lion paws. Or are you forgetting who's the monster expert here?" she said, raising an eyebrow.

Twilight cleared her throat. "So you two *think* there was a creature in your yard. But neither of you actually saw it?" Twilight clarified. Spike feverishly scribbled on a scroll. But Sweetie Belle could see he'd stopped taking notes and was now doodling what looked like a cartoon of her sister.

"Yes." Lyra and Bon Bon nodded.

"We'll look into it," Twilight reassured them as Starlight hustled the duo out of the room, bringing in Muffins.

"I was delivering packages, and a monster attacked me!" Muffins blurted.

"What kind of monster?" Twilight asked. Sweetie Belle leaned forward with interest.

Muffins was the first pony in the group who had actually *seen* a creature.

"It was big and pony-shaped, all white, with short hair!"

"That sounds a little like Bulk Biceps," Twilight said. Starlight rolled her eyes and Sweetie Belle had to smother a giggle.

"Oh no. It couldn't be him! He would have said hi! But when the monster attacked my mail cart of boxes, it went *'aaaaaghghghgh!'*"

"Definitely Bulk Biceps," Rainbow Dash muttered to the others in disgust. "Guess that explains his 'creature made of boxes.'"

Twilight thanked Muffins and told her they'd let her know when they found some answers.

"Honestly," Rarity said with a toss of her mane. "Everypony is so on edge lately.

Strange footprints? Interrupting handbells? Please."

"I'm glad nopony saw a *real* monster," Fluttershy said.

"Yup. But that was one doozy of a waste of time," Applejack said.

"Wait. You mean you're not going to investigate any of the ponies' stories?" Sweetie Belle asked.

"No point!" Rainbow Dash said. "There was obviously no real monster. Just a bunch of scaredy-ponies. Uh, no offense," she added, looking to Granny, who snorted.

"Y'all are just gonna act like nothing happened?" Apple Bloom asked.

"We'll keep our eyes open for anything strange. But what we need now is some sleep," Twilight said, stifling a yawn.

The older ponies nodded and started

toward the door. But Sweetie Belle hung back with the other Cutie Mark Crusaders.

"Some of those stories sure sounded worth checking out to me," Scootaloo told her friends. "Talk about it at school tomorrow?" Sweetie Belle and Apple Bloom nodded seriously.

After everything that had happened lately, Sweetie Belle didn't wonder *if* a scary new creature would show up in Ponyville—she wondered *when*.

CHAPTER SIX

Sweetie Belle squirmed anxiously in her seat. Today was the day Miss Cheerilee was going to cast the school play. This year, the class was doing a musical. And even more exciting, they'd be performing it in Canterlot, in front of Princess Celestia! The class fell silent as Miss Cheerilee unfurled the cast list. Sweetie Belle squeezed her eyes shut and held her breath. *Please let me get the lead role! Please let me get the lead role. Please let me get the—*

"Pip?" Miss Cheerilee asked. Sweetie Belle peeked with one eye. "You're the narrator. Diamond Tiara?" Surely Miss Cheerilee wouldn't cast *her* as the lead role, Sweetie Belle hoped.

"You'll play the Dragon Princess."

"Ew." Diamond Tiara made a face. "A Dragon? At least I get a crown."

"And, Sweetie Belle..." Miss Cheerilee said, flipping pages of her notes.

Sweetie Belle nearly bit her hooves in worry.

"You'll be our star!"

With a joyful cry, Sweetie Belle leaped out of her chair! Scootaloo and Apple Bloom jumped up, too, grinning and dancing with her.

But Miss Cheerilee wasn't done talking.

"*If* you can sing a solo for the whole class, right now."

"Of course!" Sweetie Belle smiled. Music started to play from somewhere. Sweetie Belle confidently opened her mouth to begin the opening bars...and nothing came out. She cleared her throat and tried again. This time she managed a small squeak.

Sweetie Belle's eyes darted nervously around the classroom. Snips and Snails were snickering. Twist looked at her with pity. Diamond Tiara rolled her eyes to Silver Spoon. Apple Bloom and Scootaloo gaped. But still, Sweetie Belle couldn't force out a single note! She was sure her face was turning as bright red as Apple Bloom's hair. With a whimper, she rushed out of the Schoolhouse...

To find herself in a shadowy wood. The sound of chimes echoed oddly in the weird landscape. Sweetie Belle looked around for their source, but all she could see was a large, deerlike creature stepping out of the shadows. Its body rippled like smoke, and massive wings lay folded against its back. The huge sweep of its antlers seemed almost graceful against the night sky. And then the creature turned its eyes on Sweetie Belle.

Twin white flames bored into her. She felt as if the creature could see deep into her heart. As if it could read her mind. And then, a feeling of pain, sharp and burning, seemed to engulf Sweetie Belle. She screamed...

And woke up in her bedroom, once more on the floor. Sweetie Belle panted for a moment, shaking off the terror of the nightmare. She winced as she sat up. She'd have to stop having these nightmares, or she'd be covered in bruises! But as Sweetie Belle climbed back into bed, resigning herself to another sleepless night, she wondered— had that pain she'd felt been hers... or the creature's?

CHAPTER SEVEN

The next day at the school yard, Sweetie Belle was exhausted. She was surprised to find that Apple Bloom and Scootaloo weren't very energetic, either.

"I was up late reading the newest Daring Do book," Scootaloo mumbled.

"And our chickens were makin' such a racket, I didn't get a wink-a sleep," Apple Bloom complained.

Miss Cheerilee opened the door to the Schoolhouse and cheerfully beckoned the ponies inside.

"I have a big surprise for you today, class! We're going to have auditions for our class play."

"I hope it's not a musical," Scootaloo muttered. Sweetie Belle gaped.

"What did you say?" she asked.

"Oh, just a silly dream I had," Scootaloo said, waving a hoof as if it were nothing.

"*I* had a dream about us doing a class musical, too!" Apple Bloom blurted out.

"So did *I*!" squeaked Sweetie Belle. "And I got the lead role, but I couldn't sing!"

"Did you run outside of the school into this weird, dark forest place?" Scootaloo asked.

"And see this super-strange creature made of, like, shadow, with wings and horns?" Apple Bloom added in a rush. Sweetie Belle nodded.

"And did it have—"

"*Burning white eyes?!*" all three Cutie Mark Crusaders yelled at the same time.

Their classmates shot them some frowns and odd looks.

"We musta all had the same dream!" Apple Bloom said in amazement.

"You mean nightmare," Scootaloo corrected.

"I didn't want to tell you about it, because I was afraid you'd call me a scaredy-pony again," Sweetie Belle admitted.

"Sweetie Belle." Scootaloo raised her right hoof in an earnest pledge. "We'll *never* call you that again. Promise."

Apple Bloom nodded. "Hey . . . I wonder if we're the only ponies who dreamed the same thing," Apple Bloom said. "We should ask Lilymoon and Ambermoon if they did, too. I mean, since it's about freaky creatures 'n' all."

"We'd better ask at recess," Sweetie Belle said, pointing. The rest of the class was already inside the Schoolhouse. They were late!

It seemed to take moons until recess. When it finally came, the Crusaders practically pounced on Lilymoon with their questions.

"Did you have a nightmare last night?" Apple Bloom demanded. "With a creature with antlers and wings and glowing eyes?"

"*Nooooo,*" Lilymoon said, narrowing her eyes. "Ambermoon and I never have nightmares. Auntie puts sleep charms in our pillows to keep dreams away."

"*All* dreams?" Sweetie Belle asked in surprise. She could understand not wanting nightmares, but she wasn't sure it was worth giving up good dreams.

"Yeah." Lilymoon nodded. "But tell me more about this creature. Was it all shadowy? And did it make noise when it walked?"

"Yes!" Scootaloo agreed.

"It sounded like it was ringing a bell!" Apple Bloom said at the same time.

"That's a peryton." Lilymoon frowned. "I've met some before. In fact, that's when I got my cutie mark."

"What does it mean when you see them in your dreams?" Sweetie Belle asked. Her stomach did a little flip-flop when she saw the worried look on Lilymoon's face.

"I'm not sure," Lilymoon admitted. "But when you see them in the real world—they're a warning."

"About what?" Scootaloo asked.

Lilymoon shrugged. "The best way to find out...is to ask one."

CHAPTER EIGHT

This was a bad idea, Sweetie Belle thought for probably the hundredth time. She stood in the darkness of the Everfree Forest, scattering magic herbs with the other Crusaders while Ambermoon and Lilymoon prepared the rest of the peryton summoning spell. The moon was the tiniest sliver of a hoofshaving tonight, and the air was still, almost as if the trees were holding their breaths, Sweetie Belle thought.

As Ambermoon finished painting silvery, glowing triangles on the leafy ground, Sweetie Belle squinted to look closer. At the center of the biggest triangle was...a cupcake?

"Is that part of the spell?" Sweetie Belle asked.

"Not exactly." Ambermoon frowned. "We don't have all the ingredients Auntie Eclipse's spell book says we need to call a peryton."

"Why didn't you just ask Auntie Eclipse for them?" Scootaloo shrugged.

"We kinda didn't ask permission to borrow her book...." Lilymoon admitted. "The book says we need fresh gooseberries to call a peryton. So we're using a goose feather and a strawberry cupcake."

Sweetie Belle's worry deepened. If she knew one thing about spells, it was that even the tiniest change could have a huge effect on the outcome.

"Now we need to summon the peryton with the ancient Earth pony Dance of Memory," Ambermoon said, using the glow of her horn to read from the ancient spell book. The others waited for her to go on, but she didn't.

Finally, Scootaloo prompted her.
"So . . . how do we do that?"

"It's . . . not in the book. I was hoping
Apple Bloom would know what it was,"
Ambermoon admitted.

"Just 'cause I'm an Earth pony doesn't
mean I know every kinda dance in our
history!" Apple Bloom said, miffed.

"Look. Do you want to summon this
peryton or not?" Ambermoon said irritably.

Not, Sweetie Belle thought. Maybe the
peryton nightmare didn't mean anything. And
maybe it was a coincidence that all three CMCs
had dreamed the same thing. But even as she
thought it, Sweetie Belle knew that was wrong.
Too many other things she'd heard were starting
to remind her of her dream—like Octavia
hearing bells while she was practicing and Lyra
noticing hoofprints in the garden. And Granny
Smith seeing a creature with white eyes.

With a sigh, Sweetie Belle began leaping and twirling. The others gaped at her.

"C'mon, just dance. It's better than nothing, right?" she said. With a shrug, the others joined in, except Ambermoon.

"I don't dance. Besides, somepony has to invoke the spell." Ambermoon shrugged. And with that, her glowing horn went dark.

Sweetie Belle gasped and stumbled. The Forest was now so dark, she couldn't see anything. Which was the point, she guessed.

"Peryton, watcher, guide. Guardian in shadow-hide. Come to us with answers true. Heed our call, we summon you!" Ambermoon's voice rang out across the silent Forest.

Nothing happened. As the moments stretched on, Sweetie Belle was about to make a joke about the cupcake being a *"berry"* bad substitute . . . and then she saw it.

Two white lights flickered deep in the woods. And they were getting nearer.

"The peryton's eyes," she breathed. The others turned as the bell-like chimes of its hooves grew nearer. Its shadowy body glowed silver in the darkness, a blend of a proud stag and a powerful eagle. It was beautiful, actually, Sweetie Belle thought, surprised she hadn't noticed before.

The moment was broken when Lilymoon stepped forward into the creature's path.

"Peryton. Why have you been haunting my friend's dreams? Why are you here in Ponyville? Do you bring us a message?"

The peryton didn't answer. Instead, it opened its massive wings and flapped them, blowing Lilymoon's mane into her eyes. Then with a roar, it began to buck and shake its antlers. Ambermoon shouldered Lilymoon out of the way a moment before the peryton's sharp flying hooves landed where the Unicorn had been standing.

"What's happenin'?" Apple Bloom said, a quaver in her voice.

"Why isn't it listening to you, Lilymoon?" Ambermoon demanded.

"I . . . I don't know!" Lilymoon said helplessly.

"But your cutie mark! It's about supernatural creatures, right?" Apple Bloom continued. Lilymoon stared helplessly at the peryton.

"Maybe we should get out of here," Scootaloo suggested.

Sweetie Belle agreed. But there was something about the peryton that made her feel sorry for it. She didn't think it wanted to hurt them. Instead, it seemed as if it was hurting. Or scared. She knew how that felt. And before she knew it, she was singing the rose song under her breath.

The peryton's head snapped up to look at Sweetie Belle.

"What's it doing now?" Apple Bloom hissed to Lilymoon.

"It's... listening to Sweetie Belle," Lilymoon said.

Shocked, Sweetie Belle went quiet. The peryton tossed its head in agitation, rearing on its taloned hind legs.

"Keep singing!" Ambermoon hissed.

So Sweetie Belle did, pouring all the love and reassurance into her song that Rarity always did when she sang it for her sister.

"A rose has thorns to keep it safe, but ponies have not one. A wild rose blooms where it is placed,

but ponies seek the sun." As Sweetie Belle sang, a peace came over the peryton. It slowly sank to its knees, resting. Encouraged, she continued. *"A rose is sweet and beautiful; its scent is lush and rare. But a pony's love is greater yet, and nothing can compare. So if I had to choose between a rose and pony friend, I'd throw away the flower quick and keep you till the end."*

Sweetie Belle smiled as the peryton bowed its head to her. It seemed as if the creature was thanking her.

"Scootaloo? Are you out here?" Rainbow Dash's voice rang out through the Forest.

"Sweetie Belle, darling?" Rarity's panicked call came a moment later.

"Apple Bloom! You get your hooves home right now, y'hear?" Applejack bellowed.

It was too much for the high-strung peryton. The creature leaped to its feet and bounded away into the Forest, leaving only the black night behind.

"It's our sisters! We gotta hide," Apple Bloom whispered to Lilymoon and Ambermoon. "We're not s'posta be hangin' out with you!"

"Good to know," Ambermoon said drily.

As the five young fillies huddled in hiding, Sweetie Belle couldn't help wondering about Lilymoon's cutie mark. It wasn't helpful when it came to perytons. But how could that be? It seemed Apple Bloom was thinking the same thing.

"Lilymoon? I don't mean to pry or anythin', but . . . are you sure your cutie mark is for communicatin' with creatures like perytons?"

"That's when I got it!" Lilymoon said defensively. "I was helping my family study perytons. Then it just showed up. What else could it be for?"

But the Crusaders had spent more time thinking about cutie marks than anypony, and Lilymoon's story didn't quite ring true to Sweetie Belle. She was sure they weren't getting the whole truth. And she wondered what Lilymoon was hiding.

CHAPTER NINE

None of the Crusaders was anxious to go home. They were in a heap of trouble for sneaking out. And with so many unanswered questions, they needed a place where they could work on getting answers *far away* from any lecturing sisters.

Their homes were no good, and Applejack, Rarity, and Rainbow Dash were *sure* to check the clubhouse. So finally, the friends settled on going to the Moon family greenhouse.

Sweetie Belle couldn't help but notice how upset Lilymoon looked as they crept up Horseshoe Hill. *It's all my fault*, Sweetie Belle thought. Until she'd stepped in, Lilymoon had *thought* she could control the peryton. Sweetie Belle had made a pony doubt her cutie mark: the exact opposite of what a good Crusader *should* do.

Ambermoon carefully opened the greenhouse door so it wouldn't make any noise. They sneaked inside and headed toward the back of the cavernous glass building. Sweetie Belle saw Scootaloo carefully avoid a potted plant and assumed that must be the fear fern she'd accidentally bumped into before.

"Nopony touch *that* thing," Scootaloo whispered, confirming Sweetie Belle's suspicion.

"Nopony touch *any*thing," Ambermoon added. "The fear fern isn't the only plant in here that could cause trouble."

"Seems like y'all got a lotta stuff that causes trouble," Apple Bloom observed.

"What's that supposed to mean?" Lilymoon asked defensively.

"Well..." Apple Bloom struggled to find the right words. Scootaloo, however, had no such issue.

"What's the deal with your family?" she blurted out. "The strange potions, the ancient books, the creepy plants. Your crazy aunt, and the way your dad smiles funny and your mom glares at everypony she sees." The sisters both looked shocked, then hurt, but Ambermoon's expression quickly became cold and unreadable.

"I thought you wanted to talk about the peryton, not attack our family," Ambermoon said quietly. "If we're so upsetting, maybe you should go home."

"Now, hold on," Apple Bloom said firmly. "It ain't like that! We're your friends! But you gotta admit things have been pretty crazy in Ponyville since y'all moved here. We just have some questions is all."

"What kind of questions?" Lilymoon asked. The Crusaders all glanced at one another. Where to begin?

"Well," Sweetie Belle spoke up, "what about the candy cane?"

"What are you talking about?" Ambermoon looked lost. Sweetie Belle sighed—there was no turning back now.

"Lilymoon took a candy cane from your room. She brought it to the Schoolhouse and Twist ate it. That's why she turned into a Timberwolf." Sweetie Belle watched the sisters process the information. They both looked completely baffled.

"But . . . why didn't you say anything?" Lilymoon asked as she worked things through in her head. She looked at them accusingly. "You . . . you thought . . . that we made Twist a Timberwolf on purpose?"

"Well, at that point we thought that

Ambermoon did," Scootaloo corrected her. Ambermoon's eyes widened. "That was *before* you helped with the fear fern!" Scootaloo added quickly.

"Still...a candy cane that curses the pony who eats it. That's somethin' most ponies don't have lyin' around." Apple Bloom glanced at the multitude of plants surrounding them. "Same goes for a greenhouse full of plants that do Celestia knows what."

"And then there's everything that just happened," Scootaloo added. "You said you got your cutie mark when you were studying perytons, but tonight—"

"I already *told* you I don't know what went wrong," Lilymoon blurted, on the verge of tears. "I *thought* it had something to do with supernatural creatures, but now you probably think I'm lying about that, too!" Lilymoon hid her face so nopony could see her crying. Ambermoon rushed over to comfort her sister. She glared at the Crusaders.

"Is *this* how friendship works? Accusing us of being . . . what . . . evil?"

Sweetie Belle felt terrible. She could tell Apple Bloom and Scootaloo did, too. Yes, something strange was going on in Ponyville. But Lilymoon and Ambermoon had been by their side through all of it. They had more than proven themselves . . . hadn't they?

"We asked 'cause we wanna figure it out *with* you," Apple Bloom tried to explain. "That's what friends do."

"Perhaps we don't need your kind of friendship here," a crisp voice called from the front of the greenhouse. The ponies turned to see Lilymoon and Ambermoon's mother, Lumi Nation, striding toward them. "After the way the Princess of 'Friendship' and her associates treated us, I guess I shouldn't be surprised that their younger counterparts are the same. You've all been bad influences from the start."

"Now, wait just a minute—" Scootaloo began, but Lumi cut her off.

"No, *you* wait!" The Unicorn got angrier as she spoke. "From the moment *you* three barged into this house, you've been causing trouble. You *dare* put the blame on us? You force us to answer to a princess for things that *you* have done?"

"Us?" Apple Bloom was as angry as Lumi. "All we've been doin' is tryin' to help your daughters!"

"By accusing us of some kind of evil plot? Parading us around town as malicious when it was *you* three who couldn't keep your hooves to yourselves? Well, my family has had quite enough of your help. You can see yourselves out." Lumi turned and strode out of the greenhouse. *"Girls!"* she called without looking. Ambermoon and Lilymoon looked from their friends back to their mother, then they turned and glumly followed after her.

"Come on." Apple Bloom stormed out of the greenhouse. Scootaloo and Sweetie Belle hurried after her. As they stepped into the cool night air, Sweetie Belle saw Blue Moon standing in the yard, grinning.

"You all have a pleasant evening, now," he said through his too-forced-to-be-real smile. Sweetie Belle huddled a little closer to her friends. She believed Lilymoon and Ambermoon when they said they didn't know what was going on. But she sure didn't feel the same way about their parents.

CHAPTER TEN

Sweetie Belle stared at the floor of Rarity's boutique. She was pretty certain Rarity hadn't stopped to take a breath since she had caught her sneaking in. Scootaloo and Apple Bloom were probably hearing the same from Auntie Lofty and Applejack.

"I simply *cannot* believe you, Sweetie Belle! I have been up all night, running myself ragged through the woods! I must look simply *atrocious!*" It went on like that for a long time. Rarity was furious they had sneaked out, particularly because they'd done *exactly* what Twilight and the others had told them not to. Sweetie Belle tried to explain about the peryton, but after all the differing accounts from the rest of Ponyville, Rarity didn't want to hear it. She was so angry that she sent

Sweetie Belle directly to bed and said they would discuss her punishment in the morning.

As Sweetie Belle's mind buzzed with thoughts of the peryton, the fight at Horseshoe Hill, and Rarity's lecture, it seemed as if she'd never fall asleep. But finally, her mind began to drift. One second she was going over the conversation with Lilymoon and Ambermoon, trying to think what they could have said differently, and the next, she was—

Pushing through a crowd of ponies, trying to get to the front of the stage. Songbird Serenade was about to perform!

Two large ponies blocked her view.

"Excuse me!" she called out. "I'm trying to see the stage?" The ponies turned to look down at her. It was Lumi Nation and Blue Moon! But instead of eyes, they stared at her with giant pools of shining white light! Sweetie Belle backed away from them—

And fell with a splash into the raging river! All she heard was the rush of water and the tinkling of bells.

Bells?!

Sweetie Belle looked up and saw a dark creature made of clouds galloping across the sky, blanketing the world in shadow. Instead of rain, hundreds of bells fell from the clouds, ringing all around her. She reached out and grabbed a large one as it splashed in the water.

And she was suddenly standing alone in the Ponyville Schoolhouse.

"I get it!" she said aloud. "It's a dream." The Schoolhouse looked as if nopony had been there in dozens of moons! Cobwebs stretched across the ceiling and a thick layer of dust coated every surface. The sound of bells echoed nearby. Sweetie Belle followed the sound out the front door. The peryton stood in the center of the playground.

"What should I do?" Sweetie Belle called out. The peryton cocked its head to the side. Unsure what that meant, Sweetie Belle mimicked it, cocking her head as well. The peryton trotted in place and the bells tinkled lightly. Sweetie Belle realized the peryton was *laughing* at her.

"Okay *fine*, smarty-hoof. What do you *want* me to do?" The peryton cocked its head again, more dramatically this time. Sweetie Belle's gaze followed the direction of the peryton's head to her right, where a large bell stood next to her. "*Ahhhh*. Got it." Her horn lit up as she used magic to pull the rope back and forth. The bell's chime was deep and powerful. When she looked back toward the playground, the peryton was gone. Instead, Scootaloo and Apple Bloom were there!

"That was a heckuva loud bell!" Apple Bloom said, trotting up the steps of the

Schoolhouse. Apparently, the bell had called her friends to her!

"Uh...why is the Schoolhouse gross?" Scootaloo asked, wiping dust off her hoof.

"This is a dream version. I think," Sweetie Belle explained. She thought for a minute. "Are you real Scootaloo and Apple Bloom? Or just *dream* Scootaloo and Apple Bloom?" The Crusaders considered that. Scootaloo leaped up into the air, flapping her wings. She quickly dropped and landed in a cloud of dust.

"Must be real me." She sounded annoyed. "Dream me can fly."

"Well, it's a good thing we can see one another in our sleep," Apple Bloom said with a sigh, "'cause accordin' to Applejack, I ain't leavin' my room till I'm as old as Granny Smith."

"But why are we here?" Scootaloo asked.

"I mean, who wants to hang out at school in their dreams?"

"It seemed appropriate, as I have much to teach you this night," a deep voice said from inside. The Crusaders turned. Princess Luna stood in the doorway. "I am glad you have finally arrived. Please come inside."

CHAPTER ELEVEN

"Princess Luna!" Sweetie Belle was relieved to see her. "Where have you been? I've been having super-crazy dreams! I was looking for you."

"It has been... difficult for me to reach you as of late. There are powerful magical forces in Ponyville. They are affecting the dream realm as well." The Crusaders looked at one another as they followed Luna into the Schoolhouse. If *she* was worried about what was going on in Ponyville, that meant things were worse than they thought. "An... old friend helped by leading the three of you here." Luna stood in front of the classroom in Miss Cheerilee's usual spot. "Please have a seat."

"Do we have to?" Scootaloo said, blowing a few inches of dust off a desk.

"Ah . . . allow me." Luna's horn flashed so brightly that the Crusaders had to close their eyes. When Sweetie Belle opened hers, the Schoolhouse was transformed. They stood in a cavernous room. In front of them were three desks carved from crystal, with ornate golden swirls and flourishes etched into the sides. The seats were stuffed with soft, inviting pillows. The blackboard behind Luna stretched into forever. Oversize windows lined either side of the Schoolhouse. Comets and planets floated by outside.

"Now, *this* is a classroom." Apple Bloom whistled appreciatively. Sweetie Belle made herself comfortable at one of the desks. In the past, when Luna had shown up in her dreams, things hadn't been this . . . formal. Sweetie Belle was anxious to find out what was going on. She was also nervous it would be another lecture on—

"Is this about Lilymoon and Ambermoon?" Scootaloo asked. Apparently Sweetie Belle wasn't the only one thinking it.

"Yes. And no. It is probably best to start at the beginning." The blackboard behind Luna came to life. Chalk images appeared, as if they were being drawn by some invisible force. As each drawing was completed, it began to move on its own! Sweetie Belle watched in awe as the scene animated in front of her. She recognized Princess Celestia, raising the sun. Tiny ponies at the edge of the blackboard cheered as the chalk sun rose up into the sky. And then, behind her, Princess Luna appeared. She looked angry.

"*Ooo! Ooo!* I know what's happening!" Scootaloo announced excitedly. "This is when you got jealous and...uh...you...." She trailed off, not wanting to finish her thought.

"It is all right, Scootaloo. I have made peace with my past." Luna's voice was tinged with sadness. "This is indeed *when* I became Nightmare Moon...as everypony knows. However, nopony knows *how* I became Nightmare Moon."

Sweetie Belle yelped in fright as their desks suddenly flew forward. The blackboard wrapped around Luna and the Crusaders. Chalk drawings surrounded them, becoming more detailed, more alive. It was as if they had been pulled into the past.

Sweetie Belle watched, wide-eyed, as the Luna from the past raised the moon. She looked both angry and sad. Once the moon was high in the night sky, she flew into the air and disappeared. The scene around them erased and a new one appeared: Luna flying through a world of sleeping ponies.

"As Princess of the Night, I am responsible for the realm of dreams," Luna explained. "It is a realm ruled by emotions. Fear, hope, love...jealousy, anger. The stronger the emotion, the stronger the dream." As the ponies dreamed, little bubbles of energy floated around them in different colors. Sweetie Belle assumed the different colors were different emotions. When Luna flew past them, some colors trailed after her. Bright reds, deep purples, and jet blacks. "I did not realize that my feelings about my sister were pulling at the emotions of ponies' dreams. But in my jealousy and anger, I drew more and more energy from the sleeping ponies I was meant to protect." The colors flowed around Luna, slowly changing her. She became meaner, darker, angrier.

The colors flowed together and started

to take shape. Sweetie Belle squinted, not sure what it was. The form was roundish at the top, with sharp edges at the bottom. Even though she knew it was just a drawing, the shape radiated an energy that made her tremble with fear.

"It's a helmet," Apple Bloom whispered. Sweetie Belle realized she was right. The helmet floated onto Luna's head, and the transformation was complete.

The Crusaders watched as Nightmare Moon was born.

CHAPTER TWELVE

"The Helm of Shadows." Princess Luna watched sadly as the chalk Nightmare Moon threw back her head and laughed maniacally.

"So *that's* what made you Nightmare Moon?" Sweetie Belle asked.

"Not exactly. The Helm was formed from my emotions. By using the power of dreams to build it, I made myself Nightmare Moon." The scene around them faded to darkness. "You all know the tale. Banished by my sister to the moon until I returned on the longest day of the thousandth year to bring about nighttime eternal. You also know who prevented that from happening." As she spoke, the scene shifted to the ruins of the Castle of the Two Sisters, along with drawings of ponies the Crusaders knew quite well.

"Rarity and her friends!" Sweetie Belle cheered.

Apple Bloom's eyes widened. "They look so *young*!" As they watched, the Elements of Harmony appeared by each of the ponies, and a wave of rainbow magic shot into the air, surrounding Nightmare Moon. When the magic faded, Nightmare Moon was no more, and Princess Luna had returned.

"Wow," Sweetie Belle said as the chalk ponies celebrated. "We've all heard the story, but seeing our sisters do it is..."

"Awesome," Scootaloo agreed. It was a moment each of the Crusaders had grown up hearing about.

"Look!" Apple Bloom pointed. Something off in the corner was pulsing with magical energy.

Sweetie Belle followed Apple Bloom's gaze. "The Helm of Shadows!" she squeaked.

The Helm sat off to the side, unnoticed by the celebrating ponies.

"Yes. Although your sisters and their friends freed me of my curse, the magic of the Helm was too powerful to be destroyed." As they continued watching, the sun and moon flew through the sky several times. Eventually the chalk versions of Celestia and Luna returned. "My sister and I were at a loss for what to do. The Helm was dangerous. *Anypony* who came into contact with it could be corrupted by its power." Sweetie Belle watched as Celestia and Luna carefully lifted the Helm. "We couldn't risk hiding the Helm in Canterlot or any other large city. There would be too many ponies that the Helm's dark magic could call to. So we decided to build a prison far from where anypony would dare to roam."

"The Everfree Forest," Apple Bloom

whispered. Luna nodded. As they continued to watch, magic swirled around the chalk sisters and an opening appeared in the ground. The Helm flew into the opening and plummeted for what seemed like forever.

"We buried the Helm deep in the ground, in a prison of our own design." Trees sprouted up around the cavern, their branches moving like serpents, slowly wrapping around one another. "We built a wall of living forest to keep ponies out: the Livewood. And from that living wood, we created creatures to guard the forest." Sweetie Belle shuddered as wood splintered off the trees and re-formed into hulking shapes she was all too familiar with... Timberwolves. They howled at the night sky as they circled the cavern that held the Helm. But before Sweetie Belle got *too* nervous, a familiar shadowy creature flew through the sky, wrapping itself around the Livewood, trapping most of the Timberwolves inside a blanket of shadow. Sweetie Belle heard the faint tinkling of bells.

"The peryton!" she exclaimed.

"Yes. The peryton." Luna smiled. "I summoned a creature of shadow to keep watch over the prison. And to alert me if anything ever threatened to breach its defenses." Luna turned to look at the Crusaders. "When the peryton called to me, I knew it was time to reach out to the three of you." The Crusaders looked at one another.

"Why us?" Scootaloo asked. Luna turned back at the scene in front of them, watching as the peryton rotated its head and stomped its hooves and talons. It leaped into the air and flew into the Livewood. Sweetie Belle was so tense, she could barely breathe. After a few moments, the peryton burst from the Livewood and slammed its antlers into the ground. In response, shadowy antler vines sprouted in three distinct spots. Roots, rocks, and dirt grew from the ground as if the antlers were pulling them from the earth. They formed together until three matching pillars stood next to one another. Each pillar loomed about eight feet tall and had steps twisting around it from the bottom to the top.

"*That* is why," Luna explained. "For reasons I do not know, the peryton decided to create one final lock that even my sister and I could not open. After much study, we came to believe that the only way to enter the Livewood would be to find three ponies with matching cutie marks. It was the perfect way to keep ponies away from the Helm of Shadows forever, because there have *never* been three ponies with matching cutie marks in all of Equestria's history." Luna turned to look at the Cutie Mark Crusaders. Each of their cutie marks glowed brightly. "Until you came along. Which is why *you* must protect the Livewood."

CHAPTER THIRTEEN

"...I shall be waiting for you *right* here when school lets out, so don't even *think* about going *any*where." If anything, Rarity was even more upset this morning. She had insisted on walking Sweetie Belle to school *and* walking her home afterward. But Sweetie Belle was barely paying attention to her sister, she was so preoccupied thinking about everything she had learned last night.

Was the Helm of Shadows *really* buried deep in the Everfree Forest behind a wall of living trees? And then there was that stuff about the matching cutie marks and protecting the Livewood! Did that mean that she was going to have to go *into* the Livewood? Sweetie Belle had *no* desire to go near that place.

"I just can't believe y'all." Applejack's

voice pulled Sweetie Belle's thoughts back to the present. Apple Bloom and Scootaloo were trotting toward the Schoolhouse. Applejack and Rainbow Dash followed, sharing their versions of the lecture Rarity was giving Sweetie Belle.

". . . and I told Auntie Lofty and Aunt Holiday I'd walk you home. *So no funny stuff*," Rainbow Dash finished as they reached the school. Apparently, all the Crusaders were under house arrest for the foreseeable future.

As soon as they were alone, Sweetie Belle turned to the others. "So . . . last night . . ."

"Princess Luna?" Apple Bloom asked. The others nodded.

"The Helm of Shadows?" Scootaloo shuddered. More nods.

"Did either of you say anything to anypony else?" Sweetie Belle asked. Scootaloo and Apple Bloom shook their heads.

"I wanted to make sure we all really *did* have the same dream first." Apple Bloom glanced around the room. "Have y'all seen Lilymoon?" Sweetie Belle looked around. It didn't seem as if she had arrived yet. Apple Bloom spoke quietly. "Y'know, we've heard about the Livewood before."

"We have?" Sweetie Belle asked. She couldn't remember that.

Apple Bloom nodded. "Back when we first followed Lilymoon home. Her dad said something about tryin' to break into the Livewood."

"Oh yeah!" Scootaloo scrunched up her face as she tried to recall the details. "And remember how interested they were in our cutie marks?" Sweetie Belle's jaw dropped as she realized something.

"They have matching cutie marks, too!" She looked at the others, wide-eyed.

"You mean we have to protect the Livewood from Lilymoon and Ambermoon's parents?" Scootaloo groaned. "Great..."

"But if they have matching cutie marks, why haven't they already unlocked it?" Apple Bloom wondered.

Scootaloo's wings fluttered nervously. "Does this mean Lilymoon and Ambermoon are bad guys now?" she asked. They all stared at one another.

Then Apple Bloom shook her head. "Whatever their parents are up to, I can't believe Lilymoon and Ambermoon are in on it," she said.

"Me neither." Scootaloo sighed. "But should we tell them what Luna said? How do you let somepony know her family is messing with dark magic?" Sweetie Belle wasn't sure if they should share the dream or not. Luna had told the Crusaders to protect the

Livewood . . . but what if they just ended up making things worse?

Suddenly, Sweetie Belle saw the slightest movement in the shadows accompanied by the softest chime of a bell.

"The peryton," Sweetie Belle whispered. The other two looked at her.

"What about it?" Apple Bloom asked.

"A peryton was there when Luna and Celestia buried the Helm of Shadows," Sweetie Belle said, working it out. "It made the pillars to unlock the Livewood. And Lilymoon was studying perytons—that's when she got her cutie mark. *Our* peryton showed up in Ponyville *after* Lilymoon's family moved here. I think it's the key to figuring all of this out!"

"That makes sense." Scootaloo nodded. "But . . . how can we find it? We're grounded for life!"

Sweetie Belle wished she could explain everything to her sister and let Rarity and her friends handle things. But with everything that had happened in the last couple of days, Sweetie Belle knew her sister wasn't in any mood to listen. They had to do this themselves.

"We're going to sneak off after school, find that peryton, and figure out what's really going on!" she announced. Her friends stared at Sweetie Belle in shock.

"You sure?" Apple Bloom asked.

"Not even a little bit," Sweetie Belle admitted, "but what other choice do we have?"

CHAPTER FOURTEEN

"You all realize that if we don't get any answers out here, we're in...like...the most trouble of our lives, right?" Scootaloo pushed some vines out of the way as the Crusaders traveled farther into the Everfree Forest. When class had been dismissed, Sweetie Belle and the others had hung back until Miss Cheerilee walked out to the front steps to see the class off. Then, the trio had crawled out the side window. Not the most graceful as far as escape plans went, but it had done the job.

Sweetie Belle was sure they'd get answers, but she wasn't as convinced that they'd like them. For example—why hadn't Lilymoon been at school today? She hoped nothing bad had happened to her friend.

"I got a better question," Apple Bloom said. "How are we s'posta find this peryton? Anypony remember what we're s'posta say?"

Sweetie Belle had been thinking about that. They didn't have Auntie Eclipse's spell book, or cupcakes, or any other things from the night before. But Sweetie Belle wasn't sure they needed them.

"I think we just have to find a place that's dark and quiet," Sweetie Belle said. She took in her surroundings. The trees blocked most of the late-afternoon sun. "Like somewhere over—" Apple Bloom covered Sweetie Belle's mouth and made a shushing noise. Sweetie Belle listened. She could hear ponies nearby, whispering! But before she could even think about what to do next, Scootaloo threw herself on the ground.

"*You found us!*" Scootaloo wailed. "*I'm*

sorry, Rainbow Dash! Please don't tell Auntie Lofty and Aunt Holiday! I don't want to be grounded foreverrrrrrrrrr!"

Lilymoon and Ambermoon stuck their heads out from behind a large oak tree and stared at Scootaloo.

"What are you wailing about?" asked Ambermoon.

Scootaloo jumped up and dusted herself off. "Nothing," she said quickly. "I knew it was you." The sisters joined the Crusaders. They were both wearing packs. Nopony said anything for a few seconds. Sweetie Belle could feel the tension in the air.

"We were worried when we didn't see you at school today," Apple Bloom said. Lilymoon glanced at her sister. Ambermoon nodded.

"Mother made me stay home," Lilymoon explained. "She wants to take me out of school for good."

"She told us we weren't allowed to leave the house," Ambermoon added grimly.

"So . . . what are you doing out here?" Scootaloo asked.

"Listen. You accused our family of a lot of things last night—" Ambermoon began.

"Because—" Apple Bloom tried to cut in, but Ambermoon held up a hoof to stop her.

"But you're our friends. The first friends we've had in a long time. Lilymoon and I think maybe you were right to question the things that have been going on. So when our parents left for the market, we went out to get some answers." Lilymoon used her magic to pull Auntie Eclipse's spell book out of her pack.

"We thought we would start by—"

"Finding the peryton!" Sweetie Belle finished. "Same here. We sneaked off after school. We're grounded, too."

"Well then," Ambermoon muttered, "let's get moving." She began lifting supplies out of her pack. Lilymoon opened the spell book. Apple Bloom looked at Sweetie Belle and nodded as if to say, *Speak up*. Sweetie Belle cleared her throat.

"I . . . don't think any of that is necessary," she said. The sisters stopped what they were doing.

Lilymoon glanced at her cutie mark and sighed. "I was hoping finding the peryton again would help me understand my cutie mark. But you obviously have more of a connection with it. Tell us what to do." Everypony turned to Sweetie Belle expectantly.

She wasn't sure her idea would work, but there was only one way to find out. Sweetie Belle closed her eyes.

"A rose has thorns to keep it safe," she whispered, "but ponies have not one." The Forest seemed to grow quieter around her. "A wild rose blooms where it is placed, but ponies seek the sun." She could hear the faintest tinkling of bells. "A rose is sweet and beautiful; its scent is lush and rare. But a pony's love is greater yet, and nothing can compare." The bells grew louder. "So if I had to choose between a rose and pony friend, I'd throw away the flower quick, and keep you till the end." Sweetie Belle looked up to see the peryton's glowing white eyes staring at her. It glanced at the others and pawed the ground nervously.

"Wow," Scootaloo whispered.

"Hey, Smarty-hoof," Sweetie Belle said, grinning. "We were hoping you could help us get some answers." The peryton turned and studied Lilymoon and Ambermoon, unsure.

Suddenly it leaped into the air and flew deeper into the Everfree Forest. It landed a short distance away and turned back to the fillies. The bells chimed impatiently. Sweetie Belle looked at the others. "I guess we're going that way."

CHAPTER FIFTEEN

The peryton led them deeper into the Everfree
Forest, always stopping to make sure they
were following. It was hard to distinguish the
creature from the shadows, so Sweetie Belle
relied on the constant chiming of bells to
lead her through the dark forest. She realized
she could barely see the others trotting next
to her. She glanced up and was shocked to
see stars in the sky. How long had they been
walking? She was certain none of them had
ever gone this deep into the Everfree Forest
before. Doubt began to gnaw at her.

"Hey, you okay?" Lilymoon asked,
trotting next to her.

"Yeah. Just a little nervous," Sweetie Belle
admitted.

"Why? We're just lost in a spooky forest

following a creature made of shadows, with no idea where we're going," Lilymoon said, grinning.

"Probably the Livewood," Scootaloo said. Ambermoon and Lilymoon both stopped mid-trot and looked at her with odd expressions.

"What do you know about the Livewood?" Ambermoon asked, her expression unreadable. Scootaloo looked at Sweetie Belle. Sweetie Belle wasn't sure what they should or shouldn't say. Fortunately, Apple Bloom saved them by calling out from up ahead.

"Hey, y'all! I see some kinda light!" Glad for a change in subject, Scootaloo rushed to join Apple Bloom, but Sweetie Belle watched Ambermoon and Lilymoon out of the corner of her eye. They were looking at each other with...concern? As they all approached the

light, Sweetie Belle squinted. It was bright!
Like, middle of the *day* bright! Blinded,
Sweetie Belle bumped into Apple Bloom. As
her eyes slowly adjusted, she could see they
were standing at the edge of a clearing. But
she suddenly realized she couldn't hear any
bells.

"Where's the peryton?" she asked. When
nopony responded, she turned to look at the
others. They were all staring ahead, eyes
wide. Sweetie Belle turned to see what was in
front of them.

She gasped.

It was exactly like Luna had shown them
but creepier. Sweetie Belle could see the three
antler-grown pillars in front of them, and
beyond that...

"The Livewood," Lilymoon whispered.
The branches and vines moved in a serpentine
fashion, twisting and sliding around one

another. Behind them, the glowing green eyes of Timberwolves watched the ponies intently. The peryton was nowhere to be seen. Sweetie Belle had no idea what to do next.

"Ambermoon! Lilymoon! What are you doing here?"

Sweetie Belle turned in surprise to see Lilymoon and Ambermoon's parents! Lumi Nation wore a shocked expression and Blue Moon, well...he was still grinning. They stood next to an enormous flower, its large spotted petals facing the Livewood. The blinding bright light seemed to be radiating from the flower's center.

"What are *you* doing here?" Ambermoon shot back. "You said you were going to the market!"

"I also said not to leave the house and to *stay away from those three*!" Lumi screamed.

"Answer her question, Mother," Lilymoon demanded. "What are you doing here?"

"Just an experiment, dear," Blue Moon responded calmly. "Nothing to worry you young fillies." The sudden sound of splintering wood seemed to contradict Blue Moon's sedate reply. Sweetie Belle yelped as one of the Timberwolves hurled itself against the snaking vines of the Livewood, trying to reach them. The rage on Lumi's face shifted to concern.

"Uh. They aren't s'posta be able to get outta there...right?" Apple Bloom asked nervously.

"I don't wanna find out," Sweetie Belle squeaked.

"Our work here can wait. I should get you girls home," Lumi said hastily, herding her daughters toward the Forest. "Come along, fillies. Your father will see to your friends."

"What should we do?" Scootaloo whispered as Ambermoon and Lilymoon disappeared into the darkness of the trees.

"I don't wanna stay here, but I don't trust him," Apple Bloom replied.

"At least we know *he's* not gonna eat us!" Sweetie Belle hissed.

"Good point. Let's go!" Apple Bloom said with a nod. Blue Moon stood there, grinning. He turned toward the Forest. Sweetie Belle took a step to follow him.

But something stopped her. She couldn't move her hooves!

Sweetie Belle glanced to Apple Bloom and Scootaloo in a panic. They were stuck, too!

"You three have a pleasant evening, now." Blue Moon smiled as he disappeared into the shadows of the Forest.

Sweetie Belle struggled to get free, but nothing happened. Magic held the Crusaders in place. The Timberwolves yipped in a frenzy and she heard more wood cracking. How could the Livewood have kept them trapped for so long, only to break when the Crusaders were stuck outside? Sweetie Belle heard a dry, raspy chuckle. Somepony was behind them!

"Who's there?" Apple Bloom asked.

"Help us! *Please!*" Scootaloo begged.

Auntie Eclipse walked slowly around the Crusaders, facing them. Her horn glowed brightly, holding them in place. She scowled.

"Help you?" She laughed again. "I can finally *stop* you. Permanently."

CHAPTER SIXTEEN

"Why're you doin' this?" Apple Bloom pleaded. Auntie Eclipse cackled.

"Oh no, no dearie. This isn't where I explain all my years of planning to you nosy fillies. This is where I leave you to the Timberwolves so I can carry out my plans without your constant meddling." She turned her back on them and walked toward the Forest.

"You'll *never* get the Helm of Shadows!" Scootaloo yelled. Auntie Eclipse paused. She turned back toward the Crusaders, a nasty gleam in her eye.

"Well, well, it appears you know more than you were letting on. I assume you also know about those, then?" She gestured toward the pillars. "With you three gone, I'll have the only ponies in Equestria with the ability to access the pillars' magic. I've made sure of that. So yes. I believe the Helm *will* be mine." Her raspy chuckle echoed around the clearing as she disappeared into the Forest.

Sweetie Belle couldn't see the Timberwolves. But the growling and splintering of wood behind them painted a vivid picture of what was happening.

"Anypony got any ideas?" Scootaloo asked nervously.

"Sweetie Belle, you're a Unicorn. Can't you use magic to get us free?" Apple Bloom asked. Sweetie Belle wasn't sure how to do that. But she powered up her horn anyway and tried to fight Auntie Eclipse's spell. Her hoof moved a little, but that was all.

"I can't break the magic." She panted from the effort. "Sorry."

"What about the peryton? Maybe it can help!" Scootaloo said. "Where is it?"

Sweetie Belle had no idea. But she knew how to call it.

"A rose has thorns to keep it safe," Sweetie Belle sang loudly, *"but ponies have not one. A wild rose blooms where it is placed, but ponies seek the sun."* The last time she'd used her song, she'd felt the peryton right away. This time, there was nothing...

A bell chimed. But far off.

"I heard that!" Apple Bloom yelled.

"Hello!" Sweetie Belle called into the dark. "Smarty-hoof?"

Another bell. But why did it sound so far?

A *very* loud *CRACK* distracted her. Had a Timberwolf finally gotten out? The leaves on the trees around the Crusaders started blowing wildly, accompanied by the tinkling of more bells. Sweetie Belle knew it was the peryton, but why wasn't it helping them?

"*Sweetie Belle, tell your friend we could use help, like, now!*" Scootaloo was panicking. Desperate, Sweetie Belle tried her horn again. She scrunched up her face and put everything she had into it. Her horn sparked...and suddenly she was free!

"I can move!" Sweetie Belle announced. "Maybe as Auntie Eclipse got farther away, her spell got weaker?"

"How 'bout we figure out the details later? Get us *free, please!*" Apple Bloom's voice was desperate. Sweetie Belle turned to help them—

And saw two large Timberwolves crawling out of a ragged hole in the Livewood. It was too late. She couldn't get both Apple Bloom and Scootaloo free. But she wasn't going to leave her friends behind. The Timberwolves jostled each other, trying to squeeze through the hole at the same time. Sweetie Belle's mind raced. What was different about the Livewood that was letting the Timberwolves break free now? Sweetie Belle thought back to Luna's story. The Princess sisters had grown the Livewood and created the Timberwolves, and then the peryton wrapped the Livewood in shadow....

Shadow!

Sweetie Belle knew what she had to do. She ran past her two best friends, who called after her, confused. One of the Timberwolves tore free from the gaping hole and leaped toward Sweetie Belle. But she focused on what was in front of her: the giant flower. The light was so bright, Sweetie Belle had to close her eyes. She reached out with both hooves and pulled on the flower's stem. Hard. The light sputtered. She could hear growling and smelled the Timberwolf's putrid breath behind her. With a mighty tug, she ripped the flower out of the ground.

The entire forest was thrown into complete darkness.

Sweetie Belle heard what sounded like hundreds and hundreds of bells clanging and chiming and ringing throughout the Forest. She heard the rush of wings, and her friends calling her name, and the Timberwolf's yelp. She opened her eyes, but the Forest was just as dark as if she had kept them closed. The bells continued for what seemed like forever to a scared little filly, but finally the Forest was quiet.

"Sweetie Belle?" Apple Bloom called.

"Over here!" she responded. She lit her horn so they could see her. Apple Bloom and Scootaloo rushed to her side and hugged her. Sweetie Belle looked up and saw two glowing white eyes staring down at them. "Thanks, Smarty-hoof," she said. The peryton nodded its head toward her. Sweetie Belle turned and looked at the Livewood. It was wrapped in shadow once again, the Timberwolves trapped inside. She let out a long, relieved sigh.

"How'd you know the flower was keeping the peryton away?" Scootaloo asked.

"Luna called it a creature of shadow. It can't appear in the light. I think Lilymoon and Ambermoon's family planted that solar flower to weaken the Livewood and force the peryton away. That's probably when it went and got Princess Luna in the first place." The bells chiming around them sounded like agreement to Sweetie Belle.

"Sweetie Belle, I think you may have faced off against more Timberwolves than anypony ever," Apple Bloom said in awe. Shuddering, Sweetie Belle hoped this was the last time.

"So now what?" Scootaloo asked. And for the first time since she'd seen the peryton, Sweetie Belle knew the answer.

"We have to stop the Moon family from stealing the Helm," she said grimly. "We need to talk to our sisters and their friends right away. I don't know exactly what Auntie Eclipse is planning, and I don't know if Lilymoon and Ambermoon are involved. But we'll need all the help we can get."

"Yeah! Nopony wants another Nightmare Moon on our hooves," Scootaloo said. The peryton snorted in agreement. Sweetie Belle saw a glimmer of light sneaking over the tree line. It was going to be morning soon. Their sisters would be furious, but Sweetie Belle wasn't worried. The Crusaders weren't just little fillies anymore. They were the Defenders of the Livewood.

"Let's go home," Sweetie Belle said to the others. "We've got a job to do."

EPILOGUE

As Princess Celestia finished raising the sun, Princess Luna joined her on the castle balcony. They both looked out over the land they ruled together as sisters.

"I still don't know about this," Celestia said to her sister, concern in her voice. "They are so young."

"It is not our choice to make. Forces more powerful than you or I have decided this is their burden to bear." Luna tilted her head. "Perhaps it is their youth that will be their strength."

"How so?" Celestia asked.

"The Helm sings to the darker parts of a pony's nature," Luna said. "Perhaps in their innocence, they have yet to face those darker emotions."

But Luna's words did little to comfort her sister. If anything, Celestia looked more worried than before. "Let us hope this doesn't *introduce* them to their darker natures. I would never be able to forgive us if we sent them down the path it took so long to rescue you from."

Luna had no response to that. She simply nodded. The sisters stood together, silently watching morning spread across Equestria, troubled about what the days to come would bring.